Danger is on the Thanksgiving menu at Glosser Bros. Dept. Store

By the time Jessie slipped out of the stairwell on the ground floor of the store, she was having a hard time staying calm. She was shivering, her breath coming in short, shallow bursts. She was terrified of going forward—but she had to.

Gently closing the stairwell door, she crept across the ground floor. Flashlight switched off, she looked in every direction, probing the shadows for a clue to what was happening.

CRASH!

The latest noise came from nearby, and she froze. If she stood up straight, she was sure she would have a good look at whoever was causing it.

SKRISSH!

Jessie winced as the sound of shattering glass filled the air. Gathering her courage, she got ready to leap up from behind the clothing racks for a look—but before she could, the flashlight slipped from her hand and clattered to the floor. A second later, she heard a male voice cry out in pain, and something heavy and metallic hit the floor. Then, the ground level of the Glosser Bros. Department Store fell deathly silent.

Paralyzed with fear, she stayed where she was, hunkered behind a rack of men's coats. She heard nothing, sensed no movement at all in the big room. The intruder, whoever he was, must have been as frozen as Jessie; either that, or he was incredibly stealthy. Finally, Jessie couldn't stand the suspense anymore. Retrieving the flashlight, she prepared to rise, determined to see what she could. Tensing, she counted down in her head: *three, two, one...*

This time, she sprang up, flashlight blazing in the direction of the jewelry cases...

Thanksgiving at Glosser's

By Robert Jeschonek

pie press publishing

FIRST PIE PRESS EDITION, OCTOBER 2019

Copyright © 2019 Robert Jeschonek
www.robertjeschonek.com

Cover Art Copyright © 2019 Ben Baldwin
www.benbaldwin.co.uk

All rights reserved.

This book is a work of fiction. Names, characters, places and incidents either are products of the author's imagination or are used fictitiously. Any resemblance to actual events or locales or persons, living or dead, is entirely coincidental.

Published in October 2019 by arrangement with the author. All rights reserved by the author.

A Pie Press book

ЧӀР

pie press publishing
www.piepresspublishing.com

For information about permission to reproduce sections from this book, write to piepress@piepresspublishing.com.

The text was set in Myriad Pro and Garamond.
Book design by Robert Jeschonek
ISBN-10: 0998576131
ISBN-13: 9780998576138

DEDICATION

To Alvin, Joan, Bill, and all the Glossers... Ruth and Ruby Shaffer...Mary Schuster, Loretta Nana, Dorothy Bello, Fay Frick, and all those who made us so thankful for the Glosser Bros. Department Store, Cafeteria, Hunt Room, and Snack Bar.

Jessie Preston jumped when the big box on the floor of the elevator at Glosser Bros. Department Store talked to her...though of course she shouldn't have been surprised.

The box was a friend of hers.

"Lady?" A young man's voice spoke from inside the box, muffled by the cardboard. "Yeah, you. Could you help me out, ma'am? I'm feelin' kind'a *boxed in* here."

Grinning, Jessie fell back against the wall of the elevator, combing her fingers through her short, black hair. "Oh my God, you scared me!"

The elevator dinged as it passed the second floor on the way up. The box shifted as the person inside bumped around against the sides.

"Well, you've been a good sport," he said. "Now smile! You're on *Candid Camera!*"

Jessie laughed as the lid of the box flew open and Dick Boyle popped out, grinning, his brown hair mussed. Just then, the bell dinged again, and the car stopped on the third floor. The doors slid open just in time for a heavyset woman with dark-framed horn-rimmed glasses to see the man duck back into the box. Frowning, she let the doors slide closed without stepping inside.

As the elevator started climbing again, Dick stayed in the box. "I really blew my cover, didn't I?"

"I don't know about that." Giggling, Jessie looked down into the box. "She might be too afraid to tell anyone in case they think she's crazy."

"I hope you're right." Dick held up a hand, pinching the thumb and forefinger close together. "I am *this close* to catching the *wrapping paper* bandit."

Dick, who worked in security at Glosser's, used props like the big cardboard box to disguise himself while watching for shoplifters. Most people wouldn't look twice at a box like that—but Dick could see their illegal acts quite well thanks to the eyeholes cut in the sides of the box. All it took was for a shoplifter to check out his or her loot on the elevator with Dick watching from inside his box, and the jig was up.

The bell dinged again, and the doors opened on Jessie's destination, the fourth floor. Stepping forward, she stood on the threshold, keeping the doors from sliding shut again.

"Well, I have faith in you," she said. "Like they always say, no one foils Doyle."

Dick looked over the top of the box, eyes shifting from side to side. "Nothing can stop the master of disguise," he said. "Except maybe rain or a boxcutter knife."

Jessie's dark eyes twinkled as she laughed. She loved his sense of humor, and she loved the art of disguise. He'd been teaching her about it, in fact, and all the ins and outs of department store security at Glosser Bros.

She had a flair for it, though she was only 17 years old. As for Dick, he was 25.

"See you later, box boy." She waved and stepped back out of the elevator.

"Meet me in the bargain basement at one," said Dick as he sank out of sight in the box. "*If* you can figure out where I'm hiding *this* time. Hint: it won't be inside a *box*."

With that, the doors bumped shut, and the car started back down the shaft toward the lower floors.

*****

Jessie headed straight for the personnel department, which was located among the other offices on the fourth floor. Co-workers smiled as they whisked past her on the way to errands elsewhere in the store. It was Saturday, the busiest day of the week, and the place was jumping.

Before she could reach the personnel office, however, a familiar voice called out from another office—the big one on the corner.

"Jessie Preston! Hello!"

Turning, she saw the president of Glosser Bros., Alvin Glosser, grinning in the doorway of his office. As always, he looked friendly and unassuming, a middle-aged man who could just as easily have been a salesman in one of the departments as president of the entire company.

Upbeat as ever, he waved her over and headed for his desk. "So this is the big day, isn't it?" Alvin dropped into his leather swivel chair behind the desk. "I'm going to miss seeing you around!"

Jessie frowned. "What do you mean, Mr. Glosser? I'm not going anywhere."

He frowned back, scrunching up his eyes behind his dark-framed glasses. "But I thought you were leaving us! Isn't today your last day?"

Jessie shook her head. "No, sir."

"Well, good!" Alvin reached up and scratched his head, which was mostly bald with a fringe of brown hair from ear to ear. "I'm glad to hear it! Did your dad dodge the layoff after all, then?"

Again, Jessie shook her head.

"Sorry to hear that," said Alvin. "So many people are in the same boat these days."

It was true. Thousands of workers had been cut from the steel mills in Johnstown, and the layoffs kept coming. Jessie's dad had been one of the fortunate ones, making it all the way to November 1983...but his luck had finally run out.

"I'm so sorry." Alvin leaned forward, folding his hands on the desk.

"It's all right," said Jessie. "He found a job in Buffalo."

"So your family *is* moving out of town," said Alvin.

"*They* are," said Jessie. "But *I'm* not."

Alvin looked puzzled. "You're not?"

Jessie shook her head. "I'm staying here to finish out the school year."

"Staying here?" asked Alvin. "With whom?"

"Friends." Jessie smiled. "And I'd like to keep working here, if that's okay."

Alvin grinned. "Jessie Preston, you are *always* welcome at Glosser's."

*****

When Jessie found Dick, he was in his priest outfit, rifling through dress socks on a rummage table in the bargain basement.

She couldn't help smiling when she spotted him, though she was careful not to blow his cover. For all she knew, one of the old ladies at the nearby tables might be in his crosshairs, about to be snared for shoplifting.

That was the whole reason for the disguises—to enable Dick to get close enough to shoplifters to catch them in the act. There was another reason, too, though, as Dick would be the first to admit.

It was *fun*.

Jessie appreciated *that* reason more than ever, as Dick trained her to follow in his footsteps. Sneaking around in disguise was a blast, and she loved it.

She was *good* at it, too, and that was a good thing. Her sneaking-around-the-store days were about to become a much bigger part of her life.

Though even Dick didn't know just *how* big.

"Bless you, my child." Dick saw her coming and made the sign of the cross in midair with two fingers. "Come closer, and we will pray our thanks to the Lord for these bargains."

Jessie stifled her giggles and joined him at the table. "Thank you, Father. These savings are indeed miraculous, are they not?"

"Verily," he said, and then he dropped his voice to a low whisper. "See that old lady in the black overcoat at the table by the steps?"

Without making too big a show of it, Jessie took a look. "I see her."

"She's got at least a dozen wristwatches stuffed up her sleeves," said Dick. "She just keeps pushing them up her arms when she thinks no one's watching."

"No kidding. She just looks like a law-abiding little old lady."

"Think you can take her, my child?"

Jessie shrugged. "Sure. Why do you ask?"

"How would you like to help with the bust?" asked Dick. "Your very first bust."

"Yes!" said Jessie. "As long as I don't have to get in the *cardboard box*."

"Forget the box." Dick brushed a sock through the air dismissively. "The box is in the back room. No disguises necessary for this bust, Jess."

"I like it so far!"

"It's time." Dick nodded. "Time for the little bird to leave the nest."

"Okay." He was right. He'd been training her for weeks, and it was time.

She waited another moment, until she saw the lady shove another watch up her arm under her sleeve. Then, clearing her throat, she approached her.

"Ma'am?" she said. "Please come with me."

The woman looked up from behind a pair of round spectacles. "Why is that, sweetheart? What do you need?"

"We need to talk to you about something." Jessie waved toward the door that led to the back rooms of the basement. "If you'll just come this way, please."

"If you'd just tell me, we could work it out right here." The woman spread her arms.

"It's regarding some merchandise." Again, Jessie gestured toward the back room. "Please, ma'am."

Without another word, the old lady bolted up the steps. Stunned that she could move so fast, Jessie hesitated, then charged after her.

The woman stumbled halfway up the stairs, and Jessie caught her, knocking her down. When they hit, the woman's hair flew off—it was a wig—and Jessie saw what she really looked like underneath.

She looked like a *he*.

For a second, the two of them froze, and she got a good look at him. He had blond hair and blue eyes and looked like he was in his 20s or early 30s. He actually grinned at her under the old lady makeup he had caked on his face...and then he winked.

Right before he pushed her off, scrambled back to his feet, and raced up the rest of the steps without looking back.

Jessie tumbled down the steps and hit bottom, where Dick was waiting to catch her. Both of them watched as the old lady made it up the last few steps and barreled out of the store through the doors that led to Locust Street.

"Well how do you like that?" asked Dick. "Another master of disguise!"

Jessie frowned as she dusted herself off. "That jerk!"

"Maybe so, but he was *convincing* as hell!" Dick shook his head in admiration. "I really thought he was an old lady! And it isn't *easy* to fool *me*."

"I just wish I could've caught him."

"I don't think you've seen the last of him." Dick clapped her on the shoulder. "He'll be back."

"What makes you think so?" asked Jessie.

"He's your *archenemy* now," said Dick. "*Every* hero has one!"

*****

Later, long after her shift had ended and the sun had gone down, Jessie sat behind the wheel of her beat-up olive-green Dodge Dart and ate dinner—a cheeseburger and fries from a McDonald's paper sack.

It was times like these when she really missed her family—when she was completely alone, eating dinner out of a bag by the glow of a battery-powered camping lantern in her car.

Which was parked under the carport of the house where she used to live.

Sometimes, it was so sad, she almost couldn't stand it. Just days ago, she'd been living *inside* that very house with her family, doing the things that normal 17-year-olds did.

But that was all over now. Her family was gone, starting new lives in Buffalo, New York—and she'd been left behind.

By choice.

As she nibbled the last cold fries from the bottom of the bag, she thought back to the morning when they'd left town. The rented moving truck was full and idling in the driveway, the family car hitched up behind it. Dad had stood in the dim morning light, chugging coffee, and looked at her with fatherly concern.

"Are you sure you don't want to come with us?" he'd asked.

Jessie had nodded. "I'm sure. I want to finish the school year here, with my friends."

Dad had slugged back more coffee and stared grimly up the street. "I still don't like it."

"Come on, Dad," she'd said. "You know Judy Lynne and I get along like sisters. And her mom told you herself how she doesn't mind putting me up till the end of the school year."

"I know, but..." Dad had scowled and shaken his head. "A family shouldn't split up like this."

"It's okay, Dad. We'll see each other at Christmas time."

"And I don't like not being able to pay for your room and board," Dad had told her. "We shouldn't expect the Lynnes to cover your expenses."

"Just till you get back on your feet, Dad. Isn't that what Mrs. Lynne told you?"

Dad's face had been flushed as he looked down and nodded.

"Meanwhile, I'll give them what I can from my Glosser's pay," Jessie had said. "It's all good. Don't worry about it."

Grudgingly, Dad had nodded. It had made Jessie feel good, knowing she'd taken a burden off his shoulders... given him one less thing to worry about in this difficult time.

Even if she'd had to lie to do it.

The truth was, Judy and her family were about to leave town, too, heading south. Judy's dad had just lost his own job at the Freight Car Division of Bethlehem Steel, and their family was leaving to stay with relatives in North Carolina.

Luckily, Judy's mom had trusted Jessie to tell Dad that she couldn't stay with the Lynnes after all, and Dad had been too distracted getting ready for the move and new job to check personally and make sure the arrangements were still in place. And Jessie, who wanted to stay in town no matter what and had a plan up her sleeve for doing so, kept Dad in the dark with a few white lies. It was all working out just fine.

Thinking about it had made her feel better, as sad as she'd been that day. Taking some of the burden off her father's shoulders had been a big part of the reason she'd decided to stay behind. He'd had it tough since her mom had died a year ago; the last thing Jessie wanted to do was make it tougher for him.

"Just remember," he'd told her. "If you need anything, call me. In fact, I want you to call me every day or two to catch up, all right? Just so I know you're okay."

"All right." A cool breeze had blown through the driveway, making her shiver. Fall was coming fast, and the cold weather was fast behind it.

But the thought of her father, little brother, and little sister warm and toasty in their new apartment made her feel warmer.

"Okay then, honey." Dad had held out his arms for a hug, smiling. "Wish us luck."

"Good luck." A tear had crawled down her cheek as she'd hugged him back.

"Take care of yourself," he'd said, and then he'd

broken away and headed for the truck.

Leaving her to wave and watch as it pulled away, exhaust smoke puffing into the chilly air from the tailpipe.

Thinking about that moment again made her feel sick to the stomach. So did thinking about the way things used to be in the house beside the carport.

She remembered eating dinner with her dad, her sister, Eve, and her brother, Jack. She remembered watching T.V. in the living room, brushing her teeth in the bathroom, and sleeping in her bedroom on a mattress under clean sheets and blankets.

Now, she was going to sleep in her car, wrapped up in a sleeping bag...no more than a few yards from the very house that had once been hers.

If only the realtor hadn't changed the locks and sealed the place tight. If only she could have gotten inside, returning to the little world she knew so well.

Though as empty as it was inside, it probably would have just made her feel sicker at heart.

At least she had a better life to look forward to. She had a way to get by, if she played her cards right.

Making sure the doors were locked, she crawled into the back seat of the Dart and stretched out, pulling the sleeping bag over her. She yawned and pressed her head down into the pillow, already feeling drowsy.

As she started to drift off, she hoped she'd be okay for the night. It was warm for November, in the 50s, so at least she wouldn't freeze. As long as no one bothered her, she thought she'd be fine.

After that, if her plan worked out, she wouldn't have to spend another night in her car.

The thought of it made her smile as she slept, covered by the sleeping bag under the carport of the home she'd once lived in and loved.

*****

Where was Jessie's archenemy, the criminal master of disguise? She spent most of the next day watching for him during her afternoon shift at Glosser's, to no avail.

Sometimes, she searched the store in disguise, hiding as Dick had taught her to. Other times, she hunted in plain sight, not even trying to conceal herself or what she was doing.

No matter what she tried, her archenemy wouldn't show himself. Was he lying low because he'd almost gotten caught? Or was he right in front of her, so cleverly concealed that she didn't sense his presence on any level?

Whatever he was up to, Jessie was determined to bring him in. One way or another, she would stop his shoplifting campaign and prove who the better disguise artist was.

Though it was also possible that Dick might take him down first. Sunday was supposedly Dick's day off, but Jessie kept seeing him around the store, lurking in various disguises. Coming in on his free time to hunt the bad guy was just the kind of thing Dick would do, she thought, even knowing she was on duty in his place.

She meant to ask him about it when she spotted him in the menswear department on the third floor, but she didn't get the chance. Before she could approach him, she saw a middle-aged guy stealing some neckties, and she had to cover that situation instead. She grabbed a salesman and confronted the guy, then called security on the store phone and had them send someone up to take custody of the tie-stealer...who, unfortunately, was *not* the archenemy master of disguise.

By the time the action was all over, Dick was gone.

She saw him again, later, in hardware on the fourth floor, but couldn't talk then, either. A sales associate summoned her for what turned out to be a false alarm, and Dick vanished by the time she looked for him again.

She finally gave up around 5:00—closing time—as other concerns weighed on her mind. It was the big night, after all, the test run she'd been getting ready for for weeks.

Stepping outside, she hurried down Locust Street to check on her car, which was parked in front of the offices of the *Tribune-Democrat* newspaper. She made sure the Dart was locked and safe for the night, then rushed back into the store.

After punching out at Personnel on the fourth floor, as other employees headed down in the elevators, Jessie headed up the stairs to the fifth floor.

Dick had shown her around every corner of Glosser Bros., so she knew the fifth, top floor like the back of her hand. Leaving the stairwell, she darted into the receiving department, where new stock arrived after it was shipped to the store. The place was deserted now, and she hid between boxes of merchandise in the far corner.

An hour later, when she thought the coast was clear, she emerged from her hiding place. Even then, she stayed a little longer in Receiving for good measure.

Not that she liked it much in there. The big room, with its creaky wood floors and piles of boxes, was creepy when no one else was around. To make matters worse, she bumped into something when she was backing through a dark corner and nearly screamed when she saw a human face peering back at her. Fortunately, it was only a mannequin perched on a stool, staring blankly into space. Blonde hair gleaming in the last of the day's sunlight from the windows across the room, the mannequin nearly fell until Jessie caught and restored it to its original position.

Heart pounding, she hurried out of Receiving, then, and paused outside the door, listening. From what she could hear, the top floor was entirely silent and empty.

The entire store should be just as deserted. There wouldn't even be a guard in the house; the night watchman, Steve, was in the hospital, according to Dick. The Glossers hadn't found the right person to fill in for him, so the store was temporarily unguarded at night.

Still, Jessie was nervous as she pulled the silver flashlight from her pocket and switched it on. If a watchman was on duty after all, and she got caught, she'd be in a world of trouble. In her experience, the Glosser family had only been kind and understanding, but what she was doing now might push the bounds of even their generosity.

Swallowing hard, she eased open the door to Receiving and started down the hall. As she passed the Shipping department and headed for the dim red glow of the Exit sign over the stairwell door, she heard nothing but her own footsteps. Other than the Exit sign, she didn't see a single light anywhere on the fifth floor.

Easing open the metal door, Jessie followed the beam of her flashlight into the stairwell. She closed the door carefully, then worked her way down the steps to the fourth floor.

As on the top floor, she found the fourth floor was deserted, silent, and dark. No lights were visible among the home furnishings, housewares, or paint, or under any of the office doors.

She found the same conditions on the third and second floors, though the glow of streetlights leaking through the windows brightened both levels. The ground floor was even better lit from outside, though shadows moved in the flow of headlights from passing cars on Locust and Franklin streets.

As for the Bargain Basement, it was pitch black as she gazed down into it from the top of the stairs. Chills ran up her spine as she thought of going down there, so she decided to give it a pass for now.

Turning, she threw up her arms and let out a little whoop. Finally, she was alone in Glosser's after hours. She had the entire store to herself.

Feeling a little giddy, she twirled around and danced across the floor. Though she was locked in, she felt completely free. The place was all hers, and she could do anything she wanted.

Though, of course, that wasn't *entirely* true. Whatever she did, she couldn't leave traces for anyone to find later.

And she had to be gone before anyone came to work the next day.

Humming a tune, Jessie headed for the candy and nuts counter. It was closed but not locked, and she was able to open the access doors behind the glass display case. She helped herself to a handful of cashews, just enough to quell the hunger pangs she felt. They were usually served warm, and she loved them like that...but the sweet nuts were almost as good without being heated at all.

After the cashews, she had a piece of chocolate from the back of the case, one she didn't think anyone would miss. The milk chocolate and butter cream filling were delicious.

Staying clear of the windows as much as she could, Jessie roamed the big ground floor, playing among the merchandise. In the ladies' shoe department, she tried on high heels and boots, admiring herself in the mirror. She draped herself in accessories, wrapped herself in hose, even tried on men's ties and hats and gloves. With no one around to watch—and no security cameras installed in the place—she could goof around as much as she wanted, acting like a kid playing dress-up.

Jessie ran up the stairs, then, to the second floor. (She didn't want to take the chance of using the elevators in case she got stuck.) On Two, she ran between the racks with flashlight in hand, putting on lingerie over her clothes, then throwing men's suit coats over that.

But she had the most fun on Three, where the teen girls' department was located. She tried on one outfit after another—dresses, jumpers, blouses, slacks, jackets. It was her own private fashion show, performed by the glow of her flashlight.

Eventually, though, she grew tired and took the stairs to the fourth floor. She cleaned up in the ladies' bathroom, taking a sink bath with a washrag and towel from Domestics and brushing her teeth with a toothbrush and toothpaste she'd taken from the Toiletries Department.

She'd have to bundle them up and hide them in the morning, leaving no trace of her overnight stay to be found—but she knew of the perfect spot in a far corner of the drop ceiling where she thought it unlikely that the things would be found.

Next, Jessie grabbed a pillow in Domestics and an alarm clock in Housewares and made her way to the bed that was furthest back in the furniture showroom, closest to the wall. She stretched out on it, yawning with exhaustion.

Jessie wound the clock and set it for six in the morning. According to Dick, that was a half-hour before anyone showed up for work at the store. It was early enough for her to sneak out in time to get to school by seven, as well.

With the clock ticking away at her side, she drifted off to sleep, smiling. It was good to be sleeping somewhere other than the back seat of her car.

It was *great* to be sleeping somewhere that felt like home.

*****

"Sweetie? Honey?"

At the sound of a woman's voice, Jessie stirred from a deep, deep sleep. She fought to open her eyes but couldn't; she was just too totally exhausted to manage it.

"Come on, honey. Wake up now."

She felt herself being gently shaken, and that finally did it. Jessie's eyes fluttered open, and she looked up to see a familiar face.

"There you go." The round, friendly face, surrounded by a nimbus of white hair, smiled down at her. "Wakey

wakey, egss and bakey."

"Mary?" Jessie rubbed her eyes and yawned.

"The one and only!" She was known around the store as Hunt Room Mary because she'd worked in the Hunt Room restaurant at Glosser's for decades, though she also helped in the cafeteria as well.

Shaking off the sleepiness, Jessie sat up and looked for the alarm clock. It was next to her on the bed, where she'd left it—and the time was just before six o'clock.

Clearly, she'd been misinformed about the earliest arrival of employees at Glosser Bros. Mary was there a half-hour before the first workers should have shown up, according to Dick.

"Oh no." Jessie swung her legs over the edge of the bed. "I'm so sorry."

Mary, who wore a white uniform blouse and skirt and name tag, sat down beside her. "Honey, what are you doing here at this hour? If you're the acting night watchman, you're not doing a very good job of watching the store."

"I didn't know you came in this early," said Jessie.

"Someone has to have the kitchen ready for breakfast." Mary shrugged. "I don't always come over to *this* building so early, but I had to drop off some paperwork for Accounting first thing. I'm just glad I did, because I happened to see you over here."

"Thank you, Mary. I guess I lost track of time." Jessie started to get up from the bed.

But Mary held on to her arm. "Honey, you still haven't told me why you're here right now."

Dozens of lies flickered through Jessie's mind as she wondered what to say. She didn't know Mary that well, didn't know if she could trust her—but maybe truth was her best option in the end.

"Mary, I..." What she most wanted to do was run away, but she knew she had no choice but to face up to the situation. "I needed somewhere to sleep."

"But your family..."

"Left town," said Jessie. "My dad got a job in Buffalo."

Mary frowned. "And they *left* you here?"

"I insisted. I wanted to finish the school year here, with my friends and teachers."

"And you don't have *anywhere* to stay?" Mary's frown deepened.

"No." Tears trickled down Jessie's face as she shook her head. "I thought I did, but it fell through. My friend Judy and her family had to move after her dad got laid off. Now I'm...I'm just so alone."

At the sight of Jessie's tears, Mary's expression softened. She put her arm around Jessie's shoulders and pulled her close. "Shh, it's okay. It'll be all right, honey."

"I just didn't want to sleep in my car again." Jessie let the tears and sobs come; it felt good to let it out against a sympathetic shoulder. "I thought maybe...just for a little while...I could stay *here*."

"It's against the rules, dear," said Mary.

"I know, I'm sorry."

"But...sometimes rules are made to be broken." Mary rocked a little, squeezing Jessie's arm. "As long as you're not damaging anything, and you're up and gone before the bosses get here..."

"I will be, I promise," said Jessie.

"Or maybe we could talk to the Glossers," said Mary.

"They're good people, you know. They've always helped out others in need."

"No, please." Jessie pulled away. "I don't want them to know. Can't we just keep it between *us*?"

"All right." Mary reached over and dabbed tears off Jessie's face with her fingertips. "For now, we won't tell the Glossers—but it won't be just between *us*."

"What do you mean?" asked Jessie.

Mary smiled. "I'm not the *only* one who comes in this early, and I'm not the only one who can help."

*****

The lights in the cafeteria were already shining bright when Mary led Jessie inside. The air was filled with cooking smells and the sound of pots and pans banging in the kitchen.

"Welcome to the Early Risers gang!" said Mary. "We gotta be ready for the breakfast crowd when they come through the door at eight."

Just then, the kitchen door behind the snack bar swung open, and a brown-haired woman in a white uniform emerged. She stood there, staring at Jessie—and then an identical woman in an identical uniform walked out to stand beside her.

Jessie recognized them instantly. *Everyone* who worked or shopped at Glosser's knew Ruth and Ruby, the Shaffer twins. Like Mary, they'd been working there for decades, running the snack bar, and were practically an institution.

"On your best behavior, girls! We've got company!" said Mary. "You both know Jessie, right?"

Ruth and Ruby both nodded, small smiles on their faces...though Jessie wasn't sure how well they *did* know her. She'd eaten at the snack bar many times but had never been overly friendly with either of them.

"Jessie needs a place to stay, just for a little bit," said Mary. "She'll be spending the night in the store for a while, and I told her we'd watch out for her. What do you say, girls?"

Ruth and Ruby looked at each other and seemed to come to a decision without saying a word.

"Okay," said Ruth. "As long as she doesn't cause any trouble."

"I would never do that." Jessie shook her head hard. "I promise."

"Then that's okay," said Ruby. "We believe in watching out for each other around here, don't we?"

"Glosser's is a family." Mary patted Jessie on the back. "A *crazy* one, maybe...but still *a family*. And family don't let each other down, especially at this time of the year."

"Thank you." Jessie was moved by her words. "Thank you all so much."

"Now then." Mary clapped her hands. "How about we get some food in your tummy, you poor thing? We can't have you getting so skinny, you make the rest of us *look* bad, can we?"

Jessie shook her head. "I don't want to put you out..."

"Nonsense! What say we get Dorothy to whip up some eggs and toast for Jessie here?"

Ruth and Ruby both nodded, waved, and headed into the kitchen, leaving the door swinging behind them.

"As for you..." Mary peered at Jessie from the corner

of her eye. "What time do you have to be at school, young lady?"

"Seven," said Jessie.

"And how long does it take to get there?"

"Hardly any time at all. I go to Johnstown High."

Mary nodded thoughtfully. "Then that gives you plenty of time to eat...*and* pay for your breakfast."

"Pay for it?" asked Jessie.

"No freeloaders in *this* joint, honey." Mary chuckled as she led Jessie across the cafeteria by the elbow. "I have *plenty* of potatoes for you to peel."

*****

Peeling potatoes at six in the morning was *not* Jessie's idea of fun, even using a potato-peeling machine...but she thought it was more than fair. Hunt Room Mary and the Shaffer twins could have given her the boot or turned her in; repaying their kindness with some manual labor was the least she could do.

The extra work also helped smooth the way for her to stay at Glosser's in days to come. With the restaurant ladies looking out for her, she'd be less likely to get caught...and more likely to have a full stomach.

She also wouldn't have to sneak out a window to get out of the store before business hours the way she'd planned. The snack bar, cafeteria, and Hunt Room were in a separate building called the Annex, connected to the main store building by a second-floor walkway, and Mary had a key, at least until Steve the watchman returned to duty. She could simply let Jessie out the front door of the Annex (after Jessie took a quick trip to the fourth floor of the main building to clean up in the bathroom and cover her tracks), and she'd be on her way without crawling out of a ground-level window on her hands and knees.

All in all, it seemed like the perfect arrangement. Getting caught by Hunt Room Mary had been the best thing that could have happened to Jessie.

"Breakfast's ready," said Dorothy Bello, one of the cooks, from across the kitchen. "Do you want to eat at a table or booth, dear?"

"I'll just eat back here, thanks." Jessie smiled and patted the stainless-steel table beside her.

"Okay then." Dorothy brought over the plate of eggs and toast and put it on the stainless table. "You want anything else? A cup of coffee or tea?"

"Coffee, please, with double cream and sugar." Jessie dropped her latest peeled potato in a black plastic bin and reached for the plate of food.

"Here you go. Fay will bring you your coffee." Dorothy gave her a fork and knife and smiled warmly. "And welcome to Glosser's morning family. We're glad to have you."

"Yeah, welcome!" shouted Loretta Nana, the head cook, who stomped over and grabbed the bin of peeled potatoes from her. Loretta was on the rough-and-tumble side, and Mary called her by the nickname "Gorilla." "We can always use another pair of hands around here."

"Thank you." Jessie picked up a piece of buttered toast and nibbled the corner. "It's good to be here."

"When you're done with the potatoes, how about giving me a hand with chopping the onions?" asked Loretta.

"I could use her help wiping down tables, too," said Mary as she hurried past. "Don't you be hogging her, Gorilla!"

"Will do!" Jessie smiled as she wolfed down her breakfast. Feeling wanted was a good thing. So was having food in her stomach and a place to sleep other than her car.

Her plan to stay at Glosser's was working out just fine, though she knew it couldn't last forever. Steve the night watchman would be back on the job at some point, or the Glossers would get someone to fill in for him. What Jessie would do after that, she didn't know.

But until then, at least, her new family at Glosser's was taking her mind off her old one in Buffalo.

"Save room for dessert, please." Ruth Shaffer approached with a glass parfait dish of vanilla ice cream in her hands, drizzled with fudge topping.

"Oh, thank you!" Jessie felt tears burning her eyes as she accepted the ice cream. "You really shouldn't have."

"Well, it's too late to put it back now, so enjoy." Ruth shrugged and headed back through the door to the snack bar.

Leaving Jessie to wish she could live at Glosser Bros. forever.

*****

"Are you sure you want to work *every* day, Jess?" Bill Glosser, the director of personnel (and Alvin's cousin), looked up at Jessie through a cloud of pipe smoke.

Jessie nodded from the other side of his desk. She'd gone straight to his office after school to get her schedule worked out...and, therefore, make sure she'd be in the store every evening so she could sleep on the premises. "I just wish I could work Thanksgiving Day, too."

"Well, if you're serious, maybe I could arrange to keep the store open that day." Bill smirked. "But you'd be the *only* employee on the job. Would that be okay with you?"

It *would*, but Jessie knew he was kidding. Bill was that kind of guy, always teasing—but he had a heart of pure gold.

"I guess six days out of seven will be all right," she told him.

"If that's what you want." A trim man in his mid-50s with gray-brown hair and dark-rimmed eyeglasses, Bill stared at the schedule chart on the desk in front of him. "Well, you picked a good week for it—one of the busiest of the year. Have you ever worked Black Friday before?"

"No, sir."

"It gets pretty wild. Are you sure you want to give it a try?"

"Yes, sir."

"Okey-doke then." Bill wrote her name in several boxes on the schedule, along with the shift hours she'd be assigned. Then he handed the schedule across the desk, looking up at her with eyes narrowed. "So why do you want all the work, sweetheart?"

"My dad got laid off from the mill," said Jessie. "I want to save up as much as possible so I can still pay for college."

Bill nodded as she took the schedule. "Well, that's very admirable of you. Be sure to let me know if there's anything I can do."

You just did it, she thought. "Thank you, Mr. Glosser. I will."

"Good, good," said Bill. "Have Arlene make you a copy of that and send the original back in here."

"I will." Jessie started through the door, then stopped and turned. "By the way, how's Steve the night watchman doing?"

"Better," said Bill. "Thanks for asking. You security people really stick together, don't you?"

"We really do," said Jessie, and then she left him there and headed off to start her shift in the store. She was all set now, scheduled to work almost every day of the week. That left her with just one unanswered question:

Where was she going to sleep on Thanksgiving night?

*****

"Hey, you," said the male mannequin on the display pedestal in Menswear. "Yeah, you."

Looking up, Jessie couldn't help giggling. The supposed mannequin, dressed in a white driver's cap, button-down purple silk shirt, and tight white trousers, was Dick Doyle in disguise.

Dick stood perfectly still, with one arm at his side and the other raised as if in a wave to someone he knew. His smile was frozen in place, and even his skin had a tan, plastic cast to it. Honestly, if he hadn't gotten her attention, Jessie might have walked right by, never realizing it was him.

"Dick!" she said. "What a great disguise!"

"Shhh! Don't blow my cover!" He said it in a loud whisper without visibly moving his lips. "I'm waiting to ambush your archenemy...if he ever shows his *face* in here again, that is."

"I've been looking." Jessie whispered, too. "But I haven't seen him, either."

"He has to come back," said Dick. "He can't resist the *challenge.*"

"I hope you're right." Jessie looked around but didn't see anyone who looked remotely like the other master of disguise. "I owe him some serious payback."

"I'm *ready* for him this time," said Dick. "He *won't* get away."

"I wonder if he's making the rounds at the Gee Bee stores and the Richland Mall," said Jessie. "That would explain why we haven't seen him since that first time."

"It wouldn't surprise me," said Dick.

"Should we alert security at the mall? Tell them he's working in disguise?"

"I already have. They're on the lookout."

Jessie was impressed he was a step ahead of her. "I hope they let us know if they catch him first."

"They will. One of their guards is a protégé of mine."

"Good," said Jessie. "That's good to know."

"Don't worry, we'll get him, and we'll bring him to justice. Crime doesn't pay, Jessie. *No one* is above the law."

Jessie wondered what he'd say if he knew she was living on the sly at Glosser's, eating and sleeping free of charge.

*****

That night, after Jessie's shift, things weren't quite as

free and easy as they'd been the night before. She did no dancing among the racks, didn't try on any clothes or check herself out in the mirrors. She simply waited through closing time in the Receiving department on five, picked out a magazine from the racks across from the tobacco counter on the ground floor, then got herself cleaned up for the night in the ladies' room and returned to her comfy bed in the back of the furniture showroom on Four.

Flipping through the magazine by the light of a lamp she'd set up on the bedside table, Jessie yawned, feeling exhausted. Between working in the cafeteria that morning, going to school, and working in the store that night, she'd worn herself out.

But she still felt happy. She loved the store, and she liked being among friends in her own little world. Except for the mystery of her archenemy, things were simple and relaxed there.

Her family's problems were far from her mind. So were her own thoughts of what the future might hold.

Putting aside the magazine, she wound and set the alarm clock, switched off the light, and rolled over on her side. Safe within the walls of the Glosser Bros. Department Store, she fell fast asleep, dreaming of her adventures with Dick, Hunt Room Mary, Gorilla, Dorothy, and Ruth and Ruby Shaffer—the surrogate family who were taking care of her while her real family struggled to survive in a faraway town.

*****

The next morning, after finishing her duties—and

breakfast—in Glosser's cafeteria, Jessie cleaned up, hid her things, hopped into her car on Locust Street, and drove to Johnstown High School. She only got midway through first period, though, before she was summoned to the office over the P.A. system.

"Hello?" She stepped up to the counter and spoke to the closest secretary, who was typing something. "I'm Jessie Preston. I was just called in a minute ago?"

"Good morning, Jessie." The secretary, a middle-aged woman with short brown hair, was very businesslike. According to the nameplate on her desk, her name was *Mrs. Rager.* "We called you here because there's a problem."

Suddenly, Jessie felt nervous. "What's that?"

Mrs. Rager held up a sealed white envelope. "This letter was sent to your house, but it came back undelivered."

Jessie's insides clenched as she stared at the envelope. It was a problem, all right. Her father must not have ordered mail forwarding to the new address in Buffalo.

Swallowing hard, she tried to act like nothing was wrong. "Oh, that happens sometimes. Our mailman gets confused and delivers our mail to the wrong house or returns it to the sender for no good reason."

"Really?" Mrs. Rager flapped the letter, looking suspicious.

Jessie fought to stay on an even keel. If the school found out her family had moved out of town and she was living in a department store, she was sure her happy little world would come to an end.

"Yes, it's true," she said, sounding as convincing as she could. "It drives us all crazy. Dad's registered complaints at the Post Office, but it hasn't done any good."

Mrs. Rager stared at her for another moment, giving the envelope one more flick. Then, she got up from her chair. "Well, here." She handed the letter over the counter. "I'll ask you to deliver it to your father, then."

"I'll take care of it." Jessie nodded earnestly. "Thank you."

"No problem." Mrs. Rager nodded once and returned to her desk. "Now hold on till I write you a hall pass."

"Sure." Waves of relief washed over Jessie as she waited for the pass. She'd come oh so close to being found out, but she'd dodged the danger in the end. As far as Mrs. Rager was concerned, her family just had a bad mailman.

The coast was clear...but how long would it stay that way?

*****

It must have been Jessie's day for getting called to offices.

Two hours into her shift at Glosser's that evening, she was called over the in-store P.A. to Personnel. Frowning, she broke character (as a mother-to-be, complete with baby belly, shopping in the infants' department on the third floor) and headed for Personnel on Four.

"Hi, Jessie." Bill Glosser's secretary, Arlene Goss, pointed at the phone on her desk. "There's a call for you."

"Who is it?" asked Jessie.

"Your dad." Arlene gestured at a nearby desk that was empty except for a phone. "You can take it over there."

When Jessie got to the other desk, the phone there rang. She hesitated, sitting down behind the desk, and then she picked up the receiver. "Hello?"

"Hi, Jess." It was Dad, all right. "I finally tracked you down."

"Hi, Dad." Jessie lowered her voice. "How's everything?"

"How's everything with *you*, Jess?" asked Dad. "I haven't heard a peep out of you since we left!"

"I'm good," said Jessie. "Everything's great. Just busy with school and work. You know how it is."

"Jess, are you sure everything's okay? Because I tried calling your friend, Judy Lynne, and the line was disconnected. Didn't you say you were staying with her?"

"That was just a mix-up," lied Jessie. "The bill was a little late, and the phone company cut off service."

Dad was quiet on the other end of the line. When he finally spoke, he sounded deeply concerned. "Is there anything you want to tell me, Jess? Anything you think I should know?"

"No, no," she told him. "It's all good. Nothing to worry about."

Again, he was quiet for a moment. "Do you want me to come get you, honey? I mean, it's almost the holiday anyway. You should be with your family on Thanksgiving, right?"

"Thanks, but I'm fine," said Jessie. "And I don't want to miss work. Black Friday is the biggest day of the year at Glosser's."

"Okay, then." Dad didn't sound convinced...but at least he was backing down. "But if you change your mind, let me know. Call any time, Jess."

"Thanks, Dad," said Jessie. "Now I'd better get back

to work. I'm in the middle of my shift."

"All right, honey." Dad cleared his throat. "Talk to you soon. Love you."

"Bye, Dad." Jessie hung up the phone, then lingered for a moment at the call desk. She suddenly felt her old life pressing in on her, the life of layoffs and sadness and worries. It was a life she *never* wanted to go back to.

Even so, Dad's voice echoed in the back of her mind.

*****

The next morning, Jessie woke and crawled out of bed when the alarm went off. As always, she cleaned up in the ladies' room, then gathered up and hid her things. Yawning, she made her way to the cafeteria.

"Jess honey!" Hunt Room Mary said when she walked through the door. "Am I glad to see you! Come on and help me get these tables prepped!"

"Why?" asked Jessie. "What's going on?"

"We're closed Thursday for Thanksgiving, and Thursday is always the day we serve turkey for lunch," explained Fay Frick, the gray-haired head waitress, as she pushed up a cart full of things for the tables. "Since our turkey lunches are so popular with customers, the bosses decided to serve turkey on *Wednesday* for a change. They'd rather bump our Wednesday special instead...so *everyone* will be here today. This place will be *jumping* all day!"

Jessie followed Fay and Mary's lead, arranging placemats, water glasses, and bundles of napkin-wrapped silverware on tables in the cafeteria area. "I've always loved Turkey Thursdays," she said. "My parents brought me here a lot when I was a little girl."

"I'll bet we waited on you many times," said Fay. "Ain't that something?"

"We got an employee discount." Jessie reached for more placemats from the cart. "Mom used to work at Glosser's, actually."

"She did? What's her name, dear?" asked Fay.

"Linda Preston," said Jessie. "Though you might have known her by her maiden name, Hall."

"You're Linda Hall's little girl?" Mary grinned. "Oh, hon, she was such a sweetie! She worked the perfume counter for years!"

"Thanks." Jessie placed a water glass upside-down on the top right corner of each placemat, then put the rolled-up silverware on the left side. "I just...I really miss her."

Mary's expression turned sad. "I saw the obituary, hon. I'm so sorry."

"Me, too," said Jessie.

"But you know how proud she'd be right now, don't you? If she could see you working at Glosser's like she did?"

Jessie didn't answer. Breast cancer had taken Linda too soon, but Jessie felt like a part of her was still alive within the walls of the store.

"It's not easy, I know." Mary walked over and gave her shoulder a squeeze. "This time of year, especially. But you just have to get through it."

Tears burned Jessie's eyes, and she dabbed them away.

"You just have to be grateful for the time you shared with her," said Mary. "And the family you have now. Count your blessings, hon. Try to focus on that."

"I will." Jessie sniffed, fighting off the tears.

"Keeping busy helps, too," said Mary. "In fact, I've got just the thing. Are you free at all tomorrow? On Thanksgiving Day?"

Jessie shrugged. "I guess so."

"Well, I could sure use your help." Mary winked. "It's a big project, and we need all the volunteers we can get."

"What exactly is it?" asked Jessie. "What would I be doing?"

"It's very worthwhile, hon...and it's about the same kind of work you've been doing in the kitchen already." Mary squeezed Jessie's shoulder again. "So what do you say?"

Jessie thought it over for a moment, but the decision wasn't hard. She'd already been wondering what she'd do for Thanksgiving, after all. "Okay, sure. Count me in."

*****

"Don't be so stingy with that paint," said Dick. "Go ahead and get more on your brush."

Jessie couldn't help giggling, because the can of paint he was telling her to dip into was nothing but water.

Of course, she played along, because it was all part of their undercover act. She and Dick sat atop a scaffolding on the ground floor of the store, overlooking the jewelry department. They pretended to paint a wall, when in reality, they were just brushing water around while keeping an eye on potential shoplifters in Jewelry.

"That's better," said Dick, swiping his brush up and down as he observed Jessie's technique. "Nice, even strokes. Now you're getting it."

As Jessie dipped her brush into the can for more "paint," she stole a look at a young blonde woman who was milling around the earring racks below. The woman's purse was on the counter, wide open, near the racks—the perfect spot for earrings to "accidentally" drop inside.

"So what are you doing for Thanksgiving?" Dick asked her, keeping his voice on the low side. "Any plans?"

"Helping Mary with some secret project in the cafeteria," said Jessie.

"Good for you," said Dick. "You'll have a blast."

"So what is it, exactly? Mary wouldn't tell me much."

Dick smiled as he dipped more "paint" from the can. "You'll be helping people in need. That's especially important *this* year, with all the layoffs. At the rate they're going, there won't even *be* a Bethlehem Steel in town before long."

"So you'll be volunteering, too?" asked Jessie.

Dick shook his head. "Not this year. I'll be traveling out of town. In fact, this is my last shift for a week. I'm leaving *you* in charge." Smiling, he dabbed her arm with the wet tip of his paintbrush. "But I was *really* hoping to catch your archenemy before I left." He looked down, scanning the sales floor from side to side. "I guess it'll be up to you, though. I don't see a trace of him."

"I'll do my best," said Jessie.

"You might want to focus in on the furniture showroom on Four," said Dick. "I've noticed some things missing and moved around up there."

Jessie's blood suddenly ran cold. "You have?"

"Yep." Dick nodded. "Makes me wonder if this guy is

somehow hiding out in the building."

"Wow." Jessie dipped her brush in the can again, trying not to make it too obvious that her hand was trembling. "That's hard to believe, right?"

"Maybe not," said Dick. "There are plenty of places to hide in this old store."

"Huh." Jessie's heart was hammering in her chest. Did Dick already know she was the one hiding out in the building?

"Well, do your best to find him while I'm away," he said. "Keep your eyes open for anything out of the ordinary. Not just shoplifters in disguise. *Anything*."

"I will."

"And don't worry," said Dick. "If you don't catch him, we'll do it when I get back. Steve ought to be back on night watch duty by then, so we won't be so understaffed."

"Okay, great." Jessie held her breath as she swabbed more water on the wall. Maybe Dick wasn't onto her after all...or if he was, maybe he was giving her a veiled warning that the jig was up. Either way, one thing was clear.

Her safe haven at Glosser's would soon come to an end.

*****

That evening, Jessie was extra-careful and quiet when sneaking out of her hiding place on the fifth floor and making her way downstairs. She was also more cautious than usual in retrieving the things she needed for the night and resolved not to leave the slightest trace when she put them away the next day.

She set up on a different bed, too, in the hope of throwing off anyone who might be following her trail. As careful as she thought she'd been from the start, it was time to be even more methodical in covering her tracks.

The whole thing left her troubled and uncertain of the future, unable to fall asleep. Tossing and turning on the bed, she thought about her meeting at the school office that morning, her phone call from Dad, her conversation with Mary about Mom, and Dick's warning that time was running out for whoever was hiding in the store. The alarm clock ticked loudly on the bedside table, and it seemed to her like an ominous countdown.

Maybe she'd known in her heart that her special refuge couldn't last, that she couldn't live in the Glosser Bros. Department Store forever. Maybe she'd known that at some point in the future, she would have to find another way of life somewhere else. But now, on just her fourth night sleeping at Glosser's, she realized how little time she seemed to have left in her happy little haven away from the sadness of the world.

Maybe her father had felt the same way, she thought, when he'd gotten his layoff notice from Bethlehem.

Mind racing, she continued to toss and turn, wide awake. Finally, she sat up in bed, utterly frustrated, and wondered if she could find something that would help her sleep—some warm milk, maybe, in the cafeteria.

It was then that she heard the loud bang from one of the lower floors.

Heart pounding, Jessie sat and listened, waiting for whatever came next. With any luck, if something had just fallen, there would be nothing, and she could relax.

BAM!

But she was out of luck.

For a long moment, Jessie shivered and wondered what she should do next. Maybe it was Dick down there, or Steve the night watchman had come back earlier than expected from sick leave. If someone had come to catch whoever was hiding in the store at night, she'd be in huge trouble.

But what if it wasn't security at all? What if Jessie was actually in physical danger?

CRASH!

As worried as she was, Jessie forced herself to move. She crawled off the bed, slipped on her sneakers, grabbed the flashlight, and started toward the stairs.

Maybe she could see what was going on without being noticed. Maybe she could even make it outside and run away if she had to.

Or she could always hide on the fifth floor until whoever was downstairs finally left. She thought about it as she opened the door to the stairs, thought about going up instead of down. It was probably the smart thing to do; at least it gave her a better chance of remaining undiscovered.

She almost did it, too, when she heard another bang from below—but then she decided to go down after all. As scared as she was, her curiosity compelled her to find out what was happening. Her sense of duty pushed her along, too; after all, she was still part of the Security team at Glosser's, even if she wasn't officially on the clock. If someone was breaking in, she couldn't just turn her back and run away without at least investigating and reporting the incident.

She took the stairs slowly, her sneakers softly scuffing the linoleum tile treads. When she'd descended two flights, she stopped at the door to the third floor and slowly pushed it open.

Except for the exit sign over the door and some streetlight glow from the windows, the third level was dark. Jessie ventured out a little way, watching and listening—and stopped dead when she heard another loud bang.

One thing was clear: the noise had *not* come from the third floor.

Returning to the stairwell, Jessie eased the door open and followed the beam of her flashlight down two more flights. When she peered into the shadows on the second floor, she found the same conditions as on the third. The entire level was silent and still.

BAM!

And, again, she heard noise from below.

By the time she slipped out of the stairwell on the ground floor, she was having a hard time staying calm. She was shivering, her gut twisting in knots, her breath coming in short, shallow bursts. She was terrified of going forward—but she had to.

Gently closing the stairwell door, she crouched and crept across the ground floor. Flashlight switched off so as not to draw unwanted attention, she looked in every direction, probing the shadows for a clue to what was happening.

CRASH!

The latest noise came from nearby, and she froze. If she stood up straight, she was sure she would have a good look at whoever was causing it.

SKRISSH!

Jessie winced as the sound of shattering glass filled the air. Then, it happened again.

SKRISSH!

Gathering her courage, she got ready to leap up from behind the clothing racks for a look—but before she could, the flashlight slipped from her hand and clattered to the floor.

A second later, she heard a male voice cry out in pain, and something heavy and metallic hit the floor. Then, the ground level of the Glosser Bros. Department Store fell deathly silent.

Paralyzed with fear, she stayed where she was, hunkered down behind a rack of men's coats. She heard nothing, sensed no movement at all in the big room. The intruder, whoever he was, must have been as frozen as Jessie; either that, or he was incredibly stealthy, able to move without making the slightest sound.

Finally, Jessie couldn't stand the suspense anymore. Retrieving the flashlight, she prepared to rise, determined to see what she could.

Tensing, she counted down in her head: *three, two, one.* Then, she hesitated and counted down again.

Three, two, one...

This time, she sprang up, flashlight blazing in the direction of the jewelry cases.

Her heart was in her throat as she swung the beam back and forth. If someone was over there, however, she saw no trace of him, just the glare of the flashlight on the glass cases and glittering jewelry.

Slowly, Jessie emerged from behind the rack and

crossed the floor to the jewelry department. Part of her wanted to turn around and run out of there, getting as far from the intruder as she could...but the rest of her needed to see, and know, and try—at least *try* to stop the damage to her safe haven, her happy place, her Glosser Bros.

When she reached the first of the glass cases, she looked around either side and into the middle—the square well with cases all around. Some of the cases were smashed, with shards of glass scattered around empty display stands. Other cases were undamaged and filled with jewelry, twinkling in the beam of the flashlight.

But the intruder was nowhere to be found...just shadows and racks and cases and tables, all the usual items in the middle of Glosser's ground floor.

Swinging the beam wider, she found a bare evergreen standing in the aisle—an undecorated Christmas tree. Someone had hauled it out of storage, along with cartons of ornaments and other decorations, in preparation for Black Friday. Employees would come in early that day to decorate for the Christmas shopping season, decking the halls in every conceivable way to get customers in the mood to shop.

Jessie took a deep breath and let it out slowly, guiding the flashlight's beam over the cardboard boxes stacked in the middle of the floor. The boxes overflowed with wreaths, holly, and glittering garlands; festive signs and cardboard cutout standees leaned among them.

She came to a face, then, and sucked in a startled breath—but it was only the jolly face of a full-size Santa Claus figure. Jessie recognized it from window displays of years past, suited up in the usual red cap and jacket with furry white trim.

She relaxed, scolding herself for being easily spooked.

Then, Santa suddenly lurched forward. She let out a shout of surprise as the figure crashed into her, not so harmless after all, knocking her back into one of the unbroken jewelry cases.

The flashlight dropped to the floor, and Santa's bulk pinned her against the glass. As she fought to break free, she quickly realized the figure wasn't flesh and bone, though; it was the same molded plastic Santa Claus she remembered from the window display, propelled from behind by human hands.

Slumping against the jewelry case, Jessie marshaled her strength. She shifted left, as if she were going to make a push in that direction—then lunged right with everything she had.

Her attacker was fooled, and Jessie burst free. Before he could make another move, she plowed into him, blasting him back into the cartons of decorations.

She tackled him right off his feet, knocking him into a huge carton filled with tinsel. Then, she quickly leaped away, leaving him sprawled there with his sneakered feet dangling over the edge.

"Who *are* you?" she shouted, backing away out of reach.

The man, who was masked and dressed in black, braced himself on the sides of the box and thrashed around, but he couldn't easily get out. Looking around, Jessie saw a crowbar on the floor, lit by the beam of the flashlight that had fallen nearby, and grabbed it—then swung it menacingly toward him.

With a heavy sigh, he settled back into the carton.

"I said, who *are* you?" she snapped.

Reaching up, the man pulled off the mask. "You already know."

Jessie snatched up the flashlight from the floor and aimed the beam at her captive.

Blinking at the sudden burst of light, he threw an arm up to shield his eyes. Even with his arm in the way, Jessie could see that he was older than she was, somewhere in his 20s or 30s, with a thin face and dark beard stubble. Now that she could put a face to him, he didn't seem so threatening—though she knew better than to let her guard down.

"Seriously? Don't you recognize me?" he asked.

"Should I?" asked Jessie.

The man cleared his throat, then did a bad impression of an old lady's voice. "You chased me once already, dearie. I guess you finally caught me."

Realization flashed through Jessie's brain. "You're *him*? The disguise guy?"

Her archenemy chuckled from the box, returning his voice to normal. "Yeah, that's me. Mr. Disguise."

"What's your *real* name?"

"Joe," said the man in the box. "And you're Jessie, right?"

She frowned. "How'd you know?"

Again, he chuckled. "Now what kind of master of disguise would I be if you recognized me every time I came in the store?"

Jessie's frown became a scowl. "You're telling me you were here without us knowing it?"

"Precisely."

Jessie was annoyed. "You jerk." She wanted to give him a whack with the crowbar just for tricking her like he had. "You sure went to a lot of trouble just to rob a department store."

"I had to do *something*," said Joe. "I got laid off from the mill and can't feed my *family*."

Jessie lost the edge of her anger when she heard that. His story hit close to home for her.

"*Lots* of people are laid off these days," she said. "They don't *all* rob Glosser Bros."

Joe shrugged. "What can I say? I worked here years ago and know the place inside out. I knew what to do and figured I could get away with it."

"Well, you figured *wrong*, didn't you?"

"I guess I did." Joe chuckled. "And my sources on the inside were wrong about there not being a night watchman. Though I wonder why they didn't mention you specifically?"

Jessie ignored the question. "You have sources on the inside?"

"How do you think I managed to stroll in during business hours with a crowbar up my pants leg and hide out till the middle of the night?"

"Who's your inside source?"

"An old buddy of mine, all right? Part of the cleaning crew. He's a good guy, leave him out of it." He blew out his breath. "So what do we do now, Jessie? You going to cuff me and take me in or something?"

She thought for a moment. Trying to manage him physically was a chance she wasn't willing to take, and she couldn't leave him there while she found the nearest phone and called for help. He was stuck in the box, but she figured he could smash his way free if he wanted to, in a few unguarded moments. "I guess we'll just have to wait around till someone shows up."

"Sounds boring, don't you think?" said Joe.

"I guess that depends," said Jessie, "on how boring *you* are."

*****

No, Jessie wasn't going to let him go free. It was an answer she had to give repeatedly, as Joe kept bringing it up...but eventually, he stopped asking.

The conversation was much less annoying that way. Joe told her about his family—a wife, three kids, and two dogs—and where they lived and what their lives were like. He told her about his 15-year career at Bethlehem Steel and how it had ended, leaving them all dependent on unemployment compensation and food stamps. He told her how, one day, when things had started getting bad, he'd decided on a life of crime—and he hadn't looked back ever since.

It almost made her feel sorry for having caught him. Her own path wasn't so different, really; she'd been living at Glosser's without permission, stealing (or at least borrowing) here and there to get by. She'd concealed the truth to keep from getting caught, and she'd turned to store insiders to help her with her plan.

The two of them weren't so different after all...but she still couldn't just cut him loose, even if it meant the end of her happy little world at Glosser's.

That was exactly what it meant, and she knew it. When she turned him in and reported what he'd done, she'd have to explain why she was there in the store late at night, and the full truth of her life at Glosser's would emerge. Not only would her overnight stays at the store come to an end, but she would probably lose her job. As good as the Glossers had been to her, she knew there were limits to what they'd turn a blind eye to.

To make matters worse, it didn't take long for Joe to pick up on the situation. "You weren't supposed to be here, were you?" he asked. "That's why my sources didn't give me a heads-up about you."

"You don't know as much as you think you do," she told him.

"Sure I do," said Joe. "It's *also* why we're sitting here waiting around instead of you handling this like a *real* night watchman."

Jessie yawned. "I'm getting bored talking to you after all. Maybe we should give it a rest."

"Maybe we should come to an *arrangement* instead," said Joe. "Like we *both* get out of here, and *neither* of us gets in trouble."

"No deal." She smacked the crowbar again a metal pillar. "Now shut up."

It was true, though, that she considered his offer. He didn't seem like such a bad guy, after all, and they were both in similar situations. Wouldn't she want someone to help *her* if their positions were reversed?

She was still thinking about it two hours later, at four in the morning...and then it was too late. That was when the lights came on, earlier than she'd ever known them to come on.

At which point, Hunt Room Mary walked in, stunned at the scene before her, and rushed over to help.

"Jessie!" she said. "You caught a *burglar*?"

"Why don't you ask her what she's *doing* here at four in the morning?" said Joe.

"Shut up, you," hissed Mary. "You're just mad you got caught."

"That's not it!" said Joe. "She isn't supposed to—"

Mary cut him off. "Jessie, are you okay?"

Jessie nodded. "I'm just not sure what to do with him without anyone here but us."

"Oh, don't worry, hon." Mary put an arm around her shoulders and gave her a reassuring squeeze. "Alvin and Mr. Bill will take care of this tout sweet, baby!"

*****

Mary placed a call on a phone at one of the checkouts, keeping an eye on Joe from across the store as she spoke.

Moments later, the elevator dinged, and Alvin and Bill Glosser hurried out. It was the first time Jessie had ever seen them in the store so early—and wearing white aprons over t-shirts and bluejeans, to boot.

"Happy Thanksgiving!" Alvin said it to Mary and Jessie...but then his smile became a scowl when he saw Joe. "Though not such a happy day for *you*, my friend."

"I was just trying to make ends meet after the layoff," said Joe. "Desperate times, y'know?"

It was then that Bill leaned in for a closer look at him.

"You used to work here," he said, nodding. "Years ago. You were a decent employee at the time, too, as I recall."

"Good to be remembered," said Joe.

"Sure, I remember you." Bill turned to Alvin. "His name's Joe Snyder. He was an okay guy back in the day."

"And now here you are, robbing our store." Alvin folded his arms over his chest and shook his head. "Right before Thanksgiving and Black Friday, yet."

"Bad timing," said Bill, staring Joe in the eye. "We're struggling too, you know. Folks get laid off, they don't spend as much in our store. This holiday season, we're just hoping to get back on our feet."

"Well, I'm sorry about that." Joe actually seemed contrite for the first time since Jessie had met him. "I guess I thought the insurance would cover your losses."

"Insurance doesn't cover everything, pal," said Bill. "And theft drives up our premiums. It takes money out of our pockets, and then we have less to pay our employees."

"I guess I didn't look at it like that." Joe frowned and rubbed his head. "I'm sorry. I really am."

"That doesn't solve our problem, though, does it?" asked Alvin. "Now that we've caught you, what do we do with you?"

"We have to involve the police." Bill shrugged. "We need a record of our losses and his role in the criminal activity."

"*Do* you?" Jessie was as surprised as anyone when she spoke up. "Could there be another way?"

Joe looked up at her but didn't say a word.

"What do you have in mind, young lady?" asked Alvin.

"I don't know, exactly," said Jessie. "But I don't think

he's a *terrible* person."

"Careful, Jess," Joe said sarcastically. "You don't want to go way out on a limb there."

"He's in a bad situation," continued Jessie. "Just like so many people these days."

"True," said Alvin. "But *they* didn't break into our store and smash things up, did they?"

"He made a mistake, but he did it for the right reasons," said Jessie. "I think a lot of us can identify with that."

"You're right about that, certainly." Alvin nodded thoughtfully. "And it *is* Thanksgiving."

Just then, Mary cleared her throat. "Speaking of Thanksgiving, we need to get to work in the kitchen ASAP. We're falling behind schedule on our special project, fellas."

"We are, aren't we?" Alvin smiled. "Would it help if we had an extra set of hands?" He looked at Joe.

"Yes, it would," said Mary. "Assuming those hands don't get up to no good, and the feet that go with them don't skedaddle out the door when my back is turned."

"All right then." Alvin planted his hands on his hips as he looked down at Joe. "I'm going to make you an offer, Mr. Snyder. If you don't like it, your only alternative is being turned over to the Johnstown Police."

"Shoot," said Joe. "I mean, let me rephrase that..."

"The offer is this," said Alvin. "If you join our team for the Thanksgiving special project today, we'll cut you some slack."

"Great, fine, perfect," said Joe. "That's not asking for much."

Alvin held up an index finger. "Oh, but there's more.

We need your help today, and then you'll need to work off the damages to the store after that."

Joe frowned. "You mean you're giving me a job?"

"Correct," said Alvin. "Starting Black Friday."

Bill grinned wickedly. "Working on Black Friday is a punishment in itself."

"Your pay will mostly go toward the damage you did, at least until it's repaired and paid off. Then it all goes in your pocket." Alvin reached down for a handshake. "Fair enough?"

Joe thought for a moment, then returned the handshake. "Fair enough."

Alvin looked at Jessie next. "Happy now? We did find another way."

Jessie smiled. "Happy, Mr. Glosser."

He stepped over and shook her hand, too. "And you'll notice," he said softly, "I'm not asking why certain people were here after closing time in the middle of the night when they shouldn't have been."

"Yes, Mr. Glosser," said Jessie.

"Please, call me Alvin," he said, and then he released her hand. "Now let's go, everyone. We'd better get back to the kitchen before Hunt Room Mary comes after us with a *skillet*."

*****

As soon as everyone got to the kitchen, Mary put them to work...and kept them that way.

The objective was to prepare multiple Thanksgiving dinners for early afternoon service. Other volunteers were already hard at work—including Loretta, Dorothy, Fay, the Shaffer twins, and Alvin's wife, Joan—but there was still more than enough to keep Jessie, Joe, Alvin, and Bill busy.

Basting the turkeys was one of Jessie's jobs. There were four of them in the two big ovens; they'd already been cooking for hours thanks to Loretta, who'd dropped by and gotten them started in the middle of the night. They smelled so delicious, Jessie's stomach growled as she squirted water onto their golden skins with the baster.

When she wasn't basting turkeys, Jessie helped Mary, Dorothy, and the others with peeling, boiling, chopping, and mashing sacks of potatoes. Alvin, Bill, and Joe worked harder at that than anyone, turning it into a competition to see who could mash the most in the shortest time.

Jessie worked with Loretta on the candied yams, too, laying them into trays, covering them with sauce and marshmallows, and sliding the trays into the ovens with the turkeys.

They all made vats of corn and peas, too, and mixed up huge pans of cranberry-walnut Jell-O salad and put them in the refrigerator to set.

They only stopped for a quick breakfast of scrambled eggs, toast, and coffee served in the cafeteria. They all sat around a row of pushed-together tables, chatting and laughing regardless of their station in life. Even Joe, who'd tried to rob Glosser's just hours before, was talking and eating as if he and the others were the best of friends.

Then *bam*, they were back to work in the kitchen. More potatoes were boiled and mashed, more yams were candied and baked, and more veggies were cooked. Mary and Mr. Bill made rolls from scratch and lined them up on trays, ready to bake. Joe and Dorothy made fresh green salads in big bowls and stretched plastic wrap tight as a drum over top of them.

In between basting the turkeys, Jessie helped Ruth and Ruby Shaffer fix pumpkin pies, one after another. The filling was made from fresh pumpkins delivered from Dorothy's farm in Tire Hill, spiced with nutmeg.

Everything was ready to go on schedule at noon as planned. That was when Jessie finally got to see what the rest of the Thanksgiving project entailed.

"Load 'em up, gang!" said Mary. "Let's get these goodies to the folks who need them!"

With that, the cooking team pulled everything out of the ovens and refrigerators, covered it with plastic wrap and foil, and marched outside with it. Four Glosser Bros. delivery trucks were waiting there for them, parked on Locust Street with their engines running.

The trucks were painted with brown and white stripes like Glosser Bros. shopping bags and bore the company logo on their sides. They delivered shoppers' purchases far and wide without a shipping charge of any kind, with no size limitations or restrictions.

And now they were going to deliver Thanksgiving dinner.

Bowls and trays and pans were arranged on the shelves inside each truck, held in place by cords and rails. When the loading was done, each truck carried everything needed for meals for at least one large family or several small groups.

"Move 'em out!" said Loretta. "Go feed those hungry folks!"

"You tell 'em, Gorilla!" said Mary. "Get this show on the road!"

Jessie ended up in the front seat of a truck with Alvin, who was doing the driving. He handled the truck like a pro, weaving through the streets of Johnstown as if he drove the same vehicle on the same route every day.

"This was Joan's idea, you know," said Alvin. "She's always thinking of ways to help people in need."

"Well, I think it's pretty great," said Jessie.

"Taking Thanksgiving dinner to folks affected by the layoffs." Alvin nodded. "It's the least we can do."

"I'm glad to be part of it," said Jessie. "It feels good."

"Even though your own family's been through hard times lately," said Alvin. "Good for you. That's what we call true *tzedakah*."

Jessie frowned. "What's that?"

"Acts of charity. A Jewish tradition. Our family has done good works for as long as we've lived in this town. We know how important it is to give to others."

"Cool tradition," said Jessie.

He pulled up at a stoplight then and turned to her. "But I'm sorry, that doesn't mean you can keep living at the store."

Someone must have told him the full truth, and Jessie didn't bother denying it. "I understand."

"Maybe we can figure something else out, though." The light changed, and Alvin pulled forward. "But first, let's get this food delivered and served."

*****

Jessie and Alvin served Thanksgiving dinner to a group of families at a church hall in Moxham Borough. They set up a buffet line for most of the food, with Alvin carving and dishing out the turkey at a special station.

It turned out there was more than enough to go around, so the families called in some needy friends and relations to polish it off. Soon enough, every tray, pan, bowl, and plate was empty and ready to be carted away.

Alvin and Jessie loaded the truck and returned to Glosser's Cafeteria, where Mary, Loretta, Dolores, Fay, the Shaffer Twins, and the other restaurant staff were waiting with more food (including a turkey that Mary had cooked and brought in from home). Joe Snyder was still there, too, helping with cleanup.

"C'mon, Joe." Alvin took him by the arm. "Give us a hand loading this stuff on the truck, will you?"

When they'd gotten the last of the food aboard, Alvin told him to sit up front. "You can come, too, Jessie, if you don't mind squeezing into the cab."

"I don't mind," she told him.

When the three of them had packed into the front compartment, Alvin started the truck and pulled away from the curb. "Two more stops," he said. "Then you're both home free."

The first stop turned out to be Joe's house in the West End, which surprised Jessie. Even after everything Joe had done, the president of Glosser Bros. was personally delivering Thanksgiving dinner to his family?

If also surprised Joe, who teared up when he saw where they were going. He even gave Alvin a big hug after they'd unloaded dinner and set it up in the dining room.

"Thank you," he told Alvin. "You've really given me something to be thankful for."

"That's good to know," said Alvin. "You and your family enjoy the holiday, and I'll see you Friday at the store."

The second stop was also familiar—to Jessie, this time. But Alvin didn't get out of the truck at first.

"Home sweet home," he said, smiling.

Jessie almost didn't get out of the truck, either. "My old house? But nobody's here."

Alvin gestured at the house. "Look again."

It was then that Jessie saw the rear-end of a familiar car in the carport.

"Oh my God." She saw a door open on the driver's side of that car, and a figure got out. Turning, she looked at Alvin with tears in her eyes. "How did you...? When did you...?"

"Trade secret." Alvin grinned. "Now get out there and be thankful!" He shooshed her out with a wave of his hand.

As Jessie got out of the truck, the figure emerged from the shadows of the carport. Grinning, he opened his arms wide for her.

She ran to him and let his arms wrap around her. She'd missed him more than she'd thought since he'd gone away. Living at Glosser's and being with friends like Hunt Room Mary, Gorilla, Dolores, Mr. Bill, Dick Boyle, and the Shaffer Twins had been wonderful, just what she'd needed...

But seeing her flesh-and-blood father on Thanksgiving Day was like coming home.

"I missed you, honey," said Dad. "We all did."

He turned and gestured, and the rear doors of the car

swung open. Her little sister and brother, Eve and Jack, darted out and excitedly joined the hug.

Jessie laughed. "I missed you all, too. But you shouldn't have driven all the way from Buffalo like this."

"Sure we did!" said Jack. "It's not right for a family to be apart on Thanksgiving Day!"

"That's what we're most thankful for, isn't it?" chimed in Eve. "Each other!"

"We still have that," said Dad. "No matter how tough life gets."

Jessie let her head fall against his shoulder. "But I didn't want to be a burden. I wanted to take care of myself."

"You goof." Dad patted her back. "You were more of a burden by *not* being with us. The longer we were apart, the more we worried about you."

"But I did all right, Dad," said Jessie. "With a little help from some friends."

"Good for you, honey," said Dad. "But I hope you'll consider coming home with us anyway. We *need* you, Jessie."

"No one makes us laugh like you do!" said Jack.

"And no one's as good at playing games," said Eve.

"But I'd have to change schools in the middle of the year," said Jessie. "And I'd have to find a new job and friends."

"We'll work it out," said Dad. "After what we've been through, there's nothing we can't handle together."

Jessie leaned back, wiping tears from her eyes. "Can I think about it? Today, at least?"

"Sure," said Dad. "We'll hold off going back to

Buffalo until Friday. There's just one problem. We can't exactly stay *here* tonight." He gestured at the house that had once been theirs.

Jessie turned to Alvin, who by now had gotten out of the truck and was standing nearby, listening. She couldn't exactly ask if her whole family could stay at Glosser Bros., could she? But money was tight, so a motel was out of the question, and she didn't know where else they could stay.

Alvin, fortunately, had it figured out. "If you're looking for somewhere to stay the night, you should talk to Mary," said Alvin. "When I told her your family was coming to town, she offered to put you all up."

"She did?"

"Joan and I wanted to, but Mary wouldn't take no for an answer," said Alvin. "And she already has more than enough Thanksgiving dinner cooking for *all* of you."

Fresh tears ran down Jessie's cheeks, and she dabbed them away. "Oh, thank you! I can't thank you enough!"

"Thank Mary," said Alvin. "She might not be Jewish, but she's all about the *tzedakah*."

Jessie ran over then and gave him a hug, too. As she did, she thought about her days living at Glosser's, dancing and trying on clothes and eating and sleeping in that magical place. She thought about the friends who'd helped her, and the archenemy master of disguise who'd given her a run for her money. She thought about pitching in in the kitchen and cafeteria and Hunt Room, seeing a different side of the store and the people who worked there.

And she thought about how it had helped her get back on her feet, feel better about life, and feel hopeful again about facing its challenges. She didn't feel so scared or boxed-in anymore.

Thanks to Glosser's, she felt ready to face whatever came next in her world, side-by-side with the people who loved her most.

"Happy Thanksgiving," she told Alvin. "Thank you for everything."

"Happy Thanksgiving, Jessie," he said. "*Mazel tov* to you and your family, for such a reunion is truly something to be grateful for on *any* day of the year."

ABOUT THE AUTHOR

USA Today-bestselling author and editor Robert Jeschonek grew up in Johnstown, Pennsylvania and spent many happy hours as a kid in the Glosser Bros. Department Store. Since then, he has gone on to write lots of books and stories, including *Long Live Glosser's, Penn Traffic Forever, Christmas at Glosser's, Easter at Glosser's, Halloweeen at Glosser's, A Glosser's Christmas Love Story, Valentine's Day at Glosser's, Fear of Rain, Richland Mall Rules,* and *Death By Polka* (which are all set in and around Johnstown). He has written a lot of other cool stuff, too, including *Star Trek* and *Doctor Who* fiction and *Batman* comics. His young adult fantasy novel, *My Favorite Band Does Not Exist*, won a Forward National Literature Award and was named a top ten first novel for youth by *Booklist* magazine. His work has been published around the world in over a hundred books, e-books, and audio books. You can find out more about them at his website, www.robertjeschonek.com, or by looking up his name on Facebook, Twitter, or Google. As you'll see, he's kind of crazy...in a *good* way.

ANOTHER GREAT JOHNSTOWN STORY NOW AVAILABLE FROM ROBERT JESCHONEK

ALSO AVAILABLE FROM PIE PRESS:

A GLOSSER'S CHRISTMAS LOVE STORY

BY ROBERT JESCHONEK

With her fiancé far away fighting a war in Korea, Sarah faces a blue Christmas in Johnstown, Pennsylvania in 1953. But going to work as an elf at Glosser's Department Store turns her holiday upside-down. Santa Claus, played by fellow employee Frank, falls beard over sleighbells for her. When the magic of the season at Glosser's lights a spark of romance between them, Sarah is torn between the man at war and the one in the St. Nick outfit. On the night before Christmas, she must make a fateful choice that changes everything…and leads her to a crossroads 63 years later at the famous musical Christmas tree in Johnstown's Central Park.

AND NOW, A SPECIAL PREVIEW OF A GLOSSER'S CHRISTMAS LOVE STORY…

A GLOSSER'S CHRISTMAS LOVE STORY

Johnstown, 1953

"You dropped something." The young man with the bright green eyes and red hair held up a 20-lb. frozen turkey and grinned. "Here you go."

Sarah Jensen stopped in the frozen food aisle of the Glosser Bros. grocery store and shook her head. "Not *my* turkey, thanks."

"But it is!" The guy pushed the frozen turkey toward her. "I clearly saw it fall out of the pocket of your sweater."

Sarah shrugged and sighed. She wasn't in the mood to goof around that morning, not after the letter she'd gotten before coming to work. "You must be confusing me with someone else."

"Not a chance." The guy's smile turned charming. "There's *no way* I could ever confuse you with anyone else."

The smile made Sarah hesitate. She was 23 years old,

after all, and he was...he was...

Not completely unattractive. His eyes were bright as emeralds, his hair red as firelight. He was six feet tall, with a slim, athletic build and muscular shoulders. And he was about her age or a little younger, perhaps a little older.

But no. She had her reasons for not socializing these days. And besides... "I need to get back to my register," she told him. "My lunch break is over."

"So?" He lowered the turkey, revealing the Glosser Bros. nametag pinned to the chest of his white button-down shirt. "I'm not even *on* break."

The tag, stamped with the name "Frank," caught Sarah off guard. She hadn't known he was a fellow employee. She'd never even seen him before he shoved the turkey in her face.

Not that it made any difference. "Look, I really have to get back to my register," she said.

"Then what am I supposed to do with *this?*" He turned the turkey over in his hands, looking forlorn.

It was then she was seized by the inexplicable impulse to throw him a bone. "Put it in the oven for six and a half hours at 325," she said. "Either that, or roll it down the aisle and use it to bowl for customers."

"Brilliant!" Frank perked up. "You're a genius..." He peered at the nametag pinned to Sarah's gray sweater. "...you *Sarah*, you."

"That's what they tell me." Sarah smirked. "I'm a genius, all right."

As she started to walk away, Frank stepped in front of her. "See you around?" He smiled expectantly.

"I guess so." Reaching up, she pushed a lock of her chestnut brown hair behind her right ear. "Though I've never seen you around before today."

"That's because this is my first day on the job." He winked. "But you'll be seeing me a lot more from now on."

"Is that so?" Sarah looked toward the checkouts in the front of the store. If she didn't get back to her post soon, someone would come looking for her.

"Absolutely." Frank nodded enthusiastically. "I'm like a bad penny. I keep turning up."

Sarah shrugged and headed for the checkouts. Frank backed away and disappeared in the frozen food department.

Up front, she returned to her register, apologizing for being late to the girl who'd been covering for her. The girl, a chatty redhead, didn't seem to care as she stepped away from the checkout and Sarah replaced her.

As the next customer put her items on the counter, Sarah punched their prices into the register. She slid cans of corn and green beans into the bagging area at the end of the counter, and someone caught them.

At first, Sarah didn't look to see who was doing the bagging. But as she finished ringing everything up, she turned...and there he was.

Frank Halloran himself grinned back at her as he loaded the items into big brown paper bags.

Sarah just stared. She hadn't expected to see him there.

"Ma'am?" Frank was talking to the customer. "Shall I carry these upstairs for you?" Offering to haul purchases was expected, since the grocery store was located in the basement of Glosser's department store. It was a long walk up and out to the parking lot or on-street parking, especially with a heavy load of groceries.

"Yes, please." The customer, a heavyset middle-aged

woman in a pale green coat and squat cream hat, nodded. "My car is out back in the lot." With that, she paid Sarah, got her receipt, and briskly started toward the nearby flight of stairs to the first floor.

Frank followed with a bag in each arm. He winked at Sarah as he followed the customer, mouthing four words that made her smile in spite of herself.

Penny for your thoughts?

*****

What happens next? Find out in A GLOSSER'S CHRISTMAS LOVE STORY, on sale now!

If you liked this book, you'll *love* these!

LONG LIVE GLOSSER'S

CHRISTMAS AT GLOSSER'S

EASTER AT GLOSSER'S

HALLOWEEN AT GLOSSER'S

VALENTINE'S DAY AT GLOSSER'S

PENN TRAFFIC FOREVER
(A History of the Penn Traffic Department Store)

RICHLAND MALL RULES
(A History of the Richland Mall in Johnstown)

THE GLORY OF GABLE'S
(A History of Altoona's Gable's Department Store)

FEAR OF RAIN
(A Johnstown Flood Story)

THE MASKED FAMILY
(A Cambria County Story)

**NOW ON SALE EVERYWHERE ONLINE
OR BY REQUEST AT YOUR LOCAL BOOKSTORE**
Ask your bookseller to search by title at Amazon,
Ingram, or Baker and Taylor.

Made in the USA
Columbia, SC
03 November 2019